05

Rondo in C

Also by Paul Fleischman

THE BIRTHDAY TREE
COMING-AND-GOING MEN
GRAVEN IMAGES
THE HALF-A-MOON INN
I AM PHOENIX
JOYFUL NOISE
PATH OF THE PALE HORSE
REAR-VIEW MIRRORS

Rondo in C

by Paul Fleischman

illustrated by Janet Wentworth

A CHARLOTTE ZOLOTOW BOOK

Harper & Row, Publishers   New York

So

Rondo in C
Text copyright © 1988 by Paul Fleischman
Illustrations copyright © 1988 by Janet Wentworth
Printed in the U.S.A. All rights reserved.
Typography by Patricia Tobin
10 9 8 7 6 5 4 3 2 1
First Edition

Library of Congress Cataloging-in-Publication Data
Fleischman, Paul.
    Rondo in C / Paul Fleischman ;
illustrated by Janet Wentworth. — 1st ed.
            p.   cm.
        "A Charlotte Zolotow book."
    Summary: As a young piano student plays
Beethoven's Rondo in C at her recital,
each member of the audience is stirred by
memories.
    ISBN 0-06-021856-8 : $.
    ISBN 0-06-021857-6 (lib. bdg.) : $
    [1. Piano—Performance—Fiction.   2. Stories in
rhyme.]   I. Wentworth, Janet, ill.   II. Title.
PZ8.3.F6377Ro 1988   87-29375
[E]—dc19   CIP
                                                          AC

For Dana,
con amore
P. F.

For my mother and father
J. W.

Beethoven's Rondo in C—lovely piece!

Strange how it brings to mind south-flying geese

Evenings in Mama's old house on West Twelfth

Running downhill till you can't stop yourself

The first squint of sunlight on the water in Maine

Lightning bolts! Thunder! Rain pounding the plains!

Watching Ray's train leave the station last fall

Life back in Vienna—the concerts, the balls

Falling snow swirling around the streetlight

Holding Kate close in the garden that night

Galloping bareback at dusk on Banshee

Playing this very same piece for Miss Lee

Bravo, young lady, for that Rondo in C!